A Midsummer Night's Dream

Sweet Cherry
Publishing

Published by Sweet Cherry Publishing Limited
Unit E, Vulcan Business Complex,
Vulcan Road,
Leicester, LE5 3EB,
United Kingdom

First published in the UK in 2012
2015 edition

ISBN: 978-1-78226-000-4

©Macaw Books

Title: A Midsummer Night's Dream

Lexile® code numerical measure L = Lexile® 1040L

Text & Illustrations by Macaw Books 2012

www.sweetcherrypublishing.com

Printed and bound by CPI Group (UK) Ltd, Croydon, CR0 4YY

About *Shakespeare*

William Shakespeare, regarded as the greatest writer in the English language, was born in Stratford-upon-Avon in Warwickshire, England (around 23 April 1564). He was the third of eight children born to John and Mary Shakespeare.

Shakespeare was a poet, playwright and dramatist. He is often known as England's national poet and the 'Bard of Avon'. Thirty-eight plays, one hundred and fifty-four sonnets, two long narrative poems and several other poems are attributed to him. Shakespeare's plays have been translated into every major existent language and are performed more often than those of any other playwright.

Hermia: She is young, strong-willed
and independent. She does not
hesitate to go against her father's
wishes, even in the face of death.
She is in love with a nobleman
called Lysander. She is also loved
by Demetrius, another nobleman,
but she does not return his love.

Lysander: He is a young nobleman in Athens. He is in love with Hermia, though Hermia's father does not want his daughter to marry him. Lysander believes that he will be able to convince Hermia's father, so he persuades Hermia to run away with him.

Demetrius: Demetrius, another nobleman, is the favoured son-in-law of Egeus, Hermia's father. Demetrius admitted once that he loved Hermia's friend, Helena, but later abandoned her. He pursues Hermia even though he knows she does not love him.

Oberon: Oberon is King of the Fairies. He wants to take revenge on his wife Titania, Queen of the Fairies, and his method creates confusion and humour in the play.

A Midsummer Night's Dream

Once upon a time in Athens, there was a rather strict law regarding the marriage of girls. It had been decided by the Duke that every father had the right to give his daughter's hand in marriage to a man of his choice – and if his daughter were to refuse his offer, then she would be put to

8

death. Now this law was seldom carried out, as no father wanted to see his daughter dead, but in the case of Egeus and his daughter Hermia, it was a different story altogether.

Egeus wanted Hermia to marry Demetrius, a noble youth to his liking. But Hermia knew that Demetrius had formerly professed his love for her dear friend Helena, who was madly in love with him. Of course, she did not mention that she herself was in love with a handsome man called Lysander,

but she refused to obey
her father's orders.

Theseus, the Duke of
Athens, was a noble and kind
ruler. He knew that Hermia's
decision should be respected,
but it was beyond his power to
bend the law in her favour. So
he gave her an ultimatum – she
must either marry Demetrius
in four days' time, or she
would be sent to the gallows.

Hermia now faced a
dilemma. She immediately went
to Lysander and explained the
problem to him. She told him
that she only had four days to
make up her mind, or she would
die. Lysander said that one of his

aunts lived not too far away, in a place where he knew this law would not affect Hermia, as its powers were limited to the city of Athens. He asked her to run away with him that night, and told her he would wait for her in the woods outside the city.

Hermia readily agreed to this proposal and went off

to make preparations for the
escape. However, she made
one little mistake in the whole
plan. Like the innocent young
girl that she was, she told her
friend Helena about the plan,

who went and told Demetrius.
She knew that Demetrius would
surely follow Hermia to the
woods that night, and she would
follow him. Helena was in love
with Demetrius, and to be in

the woods at night with him
was one of her oldest fantasies.

Little did everyone concerned
know that the woods were the
favourite haunt of tiny people
known as fairies. Oberon was
King of the Fairies and Titania
was his queen. They would
usually come out at midnight,
along with their entourage
of little fairies and elves.

However, during Hermia
and Lysander's flight, the King
and Queen of the
Fairies were
having a little
disagreement.
Their arguing
had continued

17

for several months, and whenever they started quarrelling, all the little elves would run away and hide out of fear.

The cause of the disagreement was that one of

Titania's friends, upon her death,
had left the Queen of the Fairies
with a small child. Oberon now
wanted Titania to give him
that little boy as a page, an idea
Titania was completely averse to.

Now, on the night in question, Titania was walking through the woods with her maids-in-waiting, when suddenly, Oberon and his merry band of men came before her. The minute Titania's eyes fell on her husband, she immediately asked her companions to leave. This infuriated Oberon, who said, "Am I not your lord, O rash fairy? Why do you cross me? Give me that little boy as my page."

But Titania merely turned her head away and replied, "Your entire

fairy kingdom cannot buy the
boy from me." This brought
greater anguish to Oberon, who
declared that before dawn the
next day, she would be begging
for his forgiveness. As Titania
left him, Oberon sent for his
favourite counsellor, Puck.

Puck was a clever and naughty sprite who would while away his time playing pranks in the neighbouring villages. He would either spoil the milk, or, using his magical powers, not allow the cream to be churned into butter. As if that were not enough, he would make people spill ale on themselves, or would pull chairs out from under people seated on them.

Oberon asked the mischievous Puck to get him a purple flower called 'Love in Idleness', the juice of which was a magic potion – when dropped on the eyelids of a person asleep, it would make them fall in love with the first person they saw upon waking up. Oberon knew of another magic potion that would make the charm created by this flower wear off, but he would not tell anyone about this until he had taken the little boy from Titania.

Puck, prankster that he
was, was overjoyed at these
new orders and rushed off
immediately. While Oberon
waited for his partner in crime
to return, he saw Demetrius
walking into the forest, followed

by Helena. He could see
Demetrius trying to ward off
Helena, insulting her at every
opportunity, but the innocent
dame kept following him.

Oberon was always friendly
towards true lovers and felt sorry

for poor Helena.
So when Puck
returned with the
flower, Oberon
ordered him to
splash some of the
juice on Demetrius' eyelids if
he could catch him asleep. All
that Puck needed to remember
was to make sure that when
Demetrius awoke, it was Helena
he saw first. As Puck left to carry
out his assignment, Oberon
walked off to find Titania.

The Queen of the Fairies
was about to fall asleep, while
the fairies were busy singing
her a lullaby. Within a few
moments, Titania was fast

asleep. Oberon walked up to
her and dropped the liquid
onto her eyelids, saying, "What
you see when you wake, do
it for your true love take."

While Oberon was trying
to convince Titania to hand over
the little boy to him through
magic, Hermia and Lysander
arrived in the woods. When
they were a short distance from
Athens, Hermia declared that she

 was very tired
and wanted
to rest for the
night. So the
two lovers
lay down
on a bed of

moss and were soon fast asleep. Just then, Puck turned up and concluded that these must be the two people his king had told him about. Without more ado, he poured the juice of the wondrous purple flower onto Lysander's eyelids and left. So, when Lysander next opened his

eyes, the first person he would see was Helena, not Hermia.

Now, it so happened that Demetrius, tired of being followed around by Helena, had started to run and was soon out of her sight. Walking sadly through the woods, Helena had come upon the sleeping pair, Hermia and Lysander. Overjoyed at finding them, she nudged Lysander to wake him up. And the magic began…

The minute he saw Helena, Lysander began expressing his love for her. Helena was naturally

shocked to hear him speak that way. She knew that he was madly in love with Hermia and thought he was making fun of her. This made her very upset. Telling him that she had not expected this, Helena ran away, tears streaming down her face, while a distraught

Lysander was left wondering what had happened. He had obviously forgotten all about Hermia, who was still fast asleep.

By the time Hermia awoke, Lysander was gone. Meanwhile, Demetrius, who was searching the forest for Hermia and Lysander, realised he was lost. Since he was very tired now, he decided to stop for a while and rest. He soon fell asleep.

Oberon, who was passing through the forest at that time, saw Demetrius

asleep. Puck had told him about the blunder and, finding the original recipient of his scheme, decided to act himself. He poured a few drops of the magical juice onto Demetrius' eyelids and left him to sleep.

When Demetrius woke up, lo and behold! The first person

he saw was Helena. As he started to give the same speech that Lysander had made to her before, Lysander arrived in search of Helena. Then they both started to woo the mystified Helena.

Hermia, who was searching the woods for her beloved Lysander, arrived and could not believe what she was seeing. Helena was now of the impression that all three of them had decided to make fun of her and she was seething. Soon the two women got into a war of words, and the men decided to find a suitable place where they could fight over Helena.

Oberon was completely taken aback by recent developments. He was furious with Puck for having messed up earlier. Puck replied that it was hardly his fault – Oberon

had merely asked him to find
two lovers, which he had done.

Oberon realised that since
he had caused this mess, it
was up to him to resolve it. He
ordered Puck to create a thick

fog over the woods immediately, which would result in all four friends losing each other. He also told Puck to lead the two men away, so that they became so tired they would be unable to walk any further. Then he gave him some juice from another plant, which would cause the effects of the purple flower to wear off. Puck was told to drop this liquid onto Lysander's eyelids, so that when he awoke

he would forget all about
Helena and go back to Hermia.

Oberon left in search of
Titania. He found her still asleep
and so dropped the magic potion
onto her eyelids. Nearby, he
found a clown asleep as well.
Through his magic, he replaced
the clown's head with that of

a donkey and woke him
up. As the foolish clown
wandered along, he came across
Titania, who was beginning to
rouse. When she saw the joker
with the donkey's head, she

immediately fell in love with him. Oberon's trick was working!

Titania immediately asked her maids to tend to the man who had completely taken over her heart. The clown, who had

no idea about the donkey's head on his shoulders, was overjoyed at the services he was being offered and decided to sleep again in comfort.

As Titania held his head in her arms and crowned it with flowers, Oberon made his appearance. He bellowed at her, accusing her of taking a donkey for a lover and being unfaithful to him. Titania was ashamed of herself, but there was little she could do. The magic had done its work.

Oberon, playing on Titania's guilt, once again asked for the boy. Obviously, the Queen of the Fairies was in no position

to fight with her husband
now that she had been caught
stroking a donkey in her arms.
So, without wasting any more
time, she immediately sent
for the boy and handed him
over to Oberon as his page.

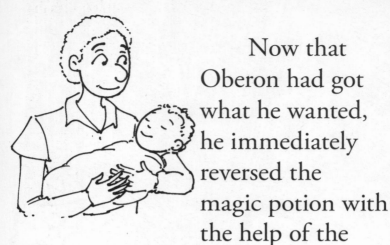

Now that Oberon had got what he wanted, he immediately reversed the magic potion with the help of the other juice and gave the clown his head back. Titania came to her senses and Oberon told her what he had done. Although Titania was angry initially, she soon relented, and the king and queen were reconciled.

Oberon then told his beloved wife about the lovers. Titania was intrigued and they set off to find the confused mortals. The royal fairies

saw that Puck had managed
to bring all four friends to
the same spot without them
knowing. Since they were now
asleep, Puck dropped the new
liquid that Oberon had given
him onto Lysander's eyelids.

Hermia was the first to wake up. She found Lysander sleeping next to her, and as she was wondering why he had suddenly started acting so strangely, he opened his eyes and saw her. He had now forgotten all about his love for Helena, and he stared

into Hermia's eyes like he
had done so many times
before. Hermia told him
what had happened to them,
but Lysander could not
remember anything. They
left together, thinking that it
all must have been a dream.

Helena and Demetrius
also woke up shortly after.
Helena was much calmer
after her restful sleep, while
Demetrius continued in
the same tone as before.
Helena thought he must be
speaking the truth and was
very happy with the way
things had turned out.

When Helena and Hermia
met again later that day, they
reconciled their differences
and were once again the best
of friends. They talked about

everything that had happened
the night before, but decided
to forget about it as they had
all got what they wanted.

Demetrius, now in love with Helena, no longer wanted to marry Hermia, so it was decided that they would all go back to Athens, where Demetrius would inform Egeus of his decision.

They hoped that would persuade
Hermia's father to repeal the
death sentence against her.
Just as they were setting off
for Athens, Egeus arrived. He
had discovered his daughter

had run away and had come to the woods in search of her.

Demetrius told Egeus that he no longer wished to marry his daughter, so Egeus could now allow Hermia to marry Lysander. Egeus declared that they would get married on the fourth day, the day on which Hermia would have been put to death. Demetrius and Helena also decided to marry on that day.

Oberon and Titania witnessed these events and were overjoyed. Oberon immediately announced a night of revelry throughout the fairy kingdom.

Acknowledgments

The editor and publishers would like to thank Mary Haselden for her help in selecting rhymes for this book and Elaine Saffer, who wrote *I like ice cream*; *The xylophone song* and *I'm going to the zoo*.

British Library Cataloguing in Publication Data

Chamberlain, Margaret
    ABC.
    I. Title
    398'.8
    ISBN 0-7214-1114-2

First edition

Published by Ladybird Books Ltd Loughborough Leicestershire UK
Ladybird Books Inc Auburn Maine 04210 USA

Printed in England

abc

illustrated by MARGARET CHAMBERLAIN

Ladybird Books

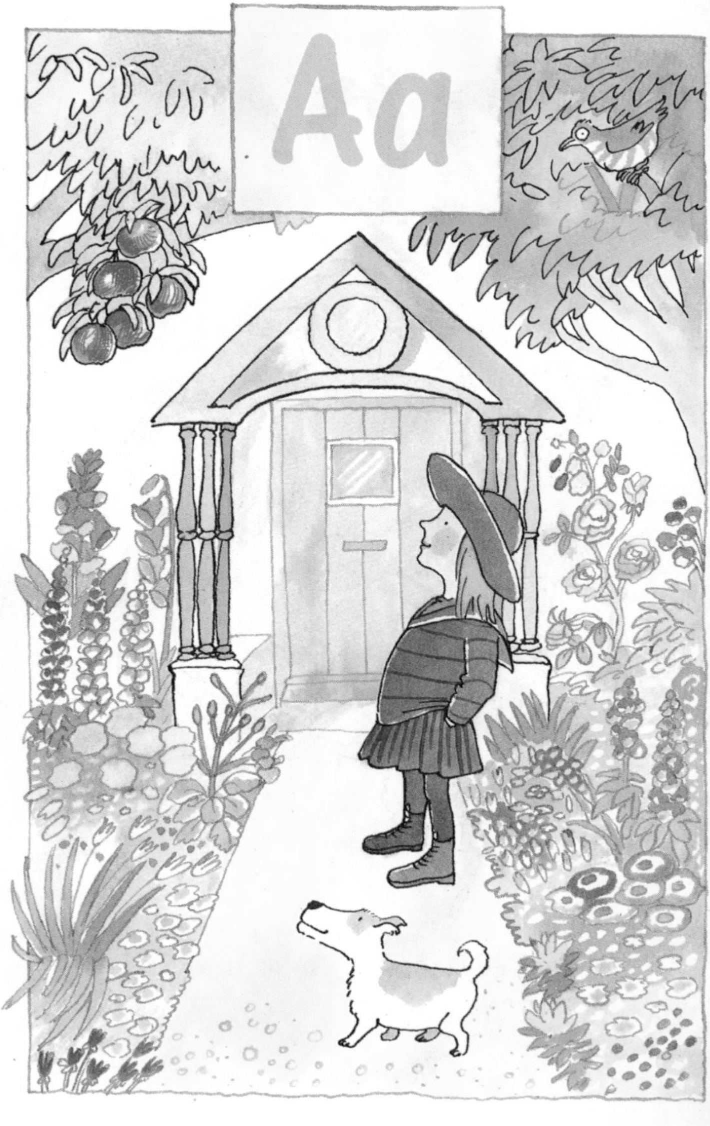
Aa

Five rosy apples by the cottage door,
One tumbled off the twig,
and then there were four.

Four rosy apples hanging on the tree,
The farmer's wife took one,
and then there were three.

Three rosy apples, what shall I do?
I think I'll have one,
and then there'll be two.

Two rosy apples hanging in the sun,
You have the big one,
and that will leave one.

One rosy apple, soon it is gone,
The wind blew it off the branch,
and now there are none.

The wheels on the bus
Go round and round,
Round and round,
Round and round.
The wheels on the bus
Go round and round,
All day long.

The horn on the bus
Goes peep, peep, peep …*etc.*

The windscreen wiper on the bus
Goes swish, swish, swish …*etc.*

The people on the bus
Bounce up and down …*etc.*

Cc

I had a little cherry stone
And put it in the ground,
And when next year I went to look,
A tiny shoot I found.

The shoot grew upwards day by day,
And soon became a tree.
I picked the rosy cherries then,
And ate them for my tea.

Miss Polly had a dolly
Who was sick, sick, sick.
So she 'phoned for the doctor
To be quick, quick, quick.

The doctor came
With his bag and his hat,
And he rapped at the door
With a rat-tat-tat.

He looked at the dolly
And he shook his head.
Then he said, ''Miss Polly,
Put her straight to bed.''

He wrote on a paper
For a pill, pill, pill;
''I'll be back in the morning
With my bill, bill, bill.''

Ee

An elephant walks like this and that,
He's terribly tall and terribly fat.
He has no fingers,
He has no toes,
But goodness gracious, what a nose!

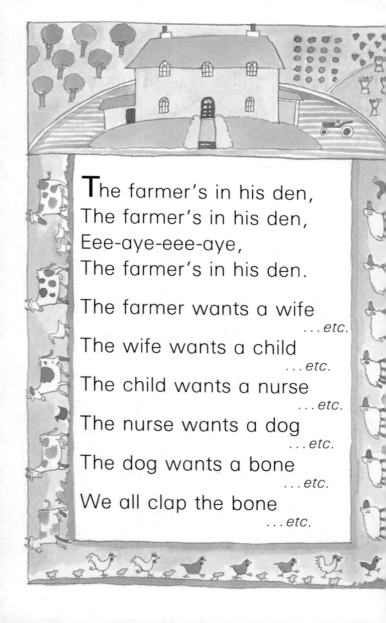

The farmer's in his den,
The farmer's in his den,
Eee-aye-eee-aye,
The farmer's in his den.

The farmer wants a wife
...etc.

The wife wants a child
...etc.

The child wants a nurse
...etc.

The nurse wants a dog
...etc.

The dog wants a bone
...etc.

We all clap the bone
...etc.

Here are Grandma's spectacles,
And here is Grandma's hat,
And here's the way
She folds her hands,
And puts them in her lap.

Here are Grandpa's spectacles,
And here is Grandpa's hat,
And here's the way
He folds his arms,
And takes a little nap.

Raise your hands above your head,
Clap them one, two, three;
Rest them now upon your hips,
Slowly bend your knees.

Up again and stand up tall,
Put your right foot out;
Shake your fingers, nod your head,
And twist yourself about.

I like ice cream,
It's my favourite treat.
I like ice cream,
That's what I like to eat.
And I like ice cream any time I can.
Oh, I like ice cream,
Here's the ice cream man.

Jj

Jack-in-the-box...
Jumps up like this!
He makes me laugh
As he waggles his head.
I gently press him down again
Saying, ''Jack-in-the-box,
You must go to bed.''

Old King Cole
Was a merry old soul,
And a merry old soul was he;
He called for his pipe,
And he called for his bowl,
And he called for his fiddlers three.

Ladybird, ladybird,
Fly away home,
Your house is on fire
And your children all gone;
All except one
And that's little Ann
And she's crept under
The frying pan.

There's such a tiny little mouse,
Living safely in my house.
Out at night he'll softly creep,
When everyone is fast asleep;
But always in the light of day
He'll softly, softly creep away.

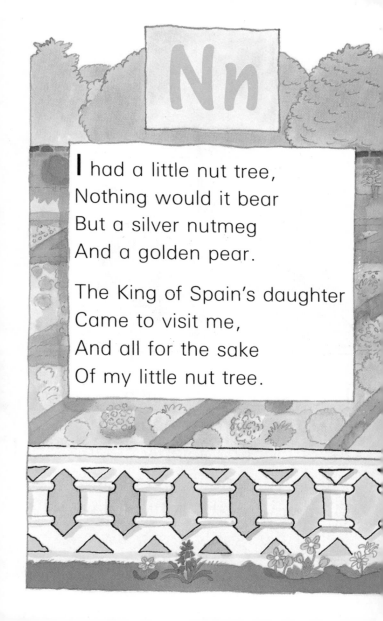

Nn

I had a little nut tree,
Nothing would it bear
But a silver nutmeg
And a golden pear.

The King of Spain's daughter
Came to visit me,
And all for the sake
Of my little nut tree.

Oo

"**O**ranges and lemons,"
Say the bells of St Clements.

"You owe me five farthings,"
Say the bells of St Martins.

"When will you pay me?"
Say the bells of Old Bailey.

"When I grow rich,"
Say the bells at Shoreditch.

"When will that be?"
Say the bells of Stepney.

"I'm sure I don't know,"
Says the great bell at Bow.

Here comes the candle
    to light you to bed,
Here comes the chopper
    to chop off your head.
Chip, chop, chip, chop
    the last man's...head.

P p

Five little peas
      in a peapod pressed;
One grew, two grew
      and so did all the rest.
They grew and grew
      and did not stop,
Until one day the peapod popped.

Qq

The Queen of Hearts
She made some tarts,
All on a summer's day.
The Knave of Hearts
He stole those tarts,
And took them clean away.

The King of Hearts
Called for the tarts,
And beat the knave full sore.
The Knave of Hearts
Brought back the tarts,
And vowed he'd steal no more.

Ring a ring o' roses,
A pocket full of posies,
A-tishoo, a-tishoo,
We all fall down.

The king has sent his daughter
To fetch a pail of water,
A-tishoo, a-tishoo,
We all fall down.

The robin on the steeple
Is singing to the people,
A-tishoo, a-tishoo,
We all fall down.

I saw a slippery, slithery snake
Slide through the grasses,
Making them shake.

He looked at me with his beady eye.
''Go away from my
Pretty green garden,'' said I.

''SSS,'' said the slippery,
                         slithery snake,
As he slid through the grasses,
Making them shake.

The tortoise can't go out to play
Or sell his house or rent it;
For when he moves,
His house moves too
And nothing can prevent it.

Uu

Please open your umbrella,
Please open your umbrella,
Please open your umbrella,
And shield me from the rain.

The shower is nearly over,
The shower is nearly over,
The shower is nearly over,
So shut it up again.

There's a worm
At the bottom of the garden,
And his name is Wiggly Woo.
There's a worm
At the bottom of the garden,
And all that he can do,
Is to wiggle all night,
And wiggle all day.
Whatever else the folk may say,
There's a worm
At the bottom of the garden,
And his name is Wiggly,
Wig, Wig, Wiggly,
Wig, Wig, Wiggly Woo, oo, oo.

Last year for my birthday
I got a xylophone.
Although I couldn't play it,
I learnt how on my own.
Now I know some music
And I love the bouncy tone.
So I play for hours each day
Upon my xylophone.

Yankee Doodle came to town,
Riding on a pony;
He stuck a feather in his cap
And called it Macaroni.

I'm going to the zoo,
Going to the zoo.
I'll see lions and tigers,
And a jumping kangaroo.
I'm going to the zoo.
There'll be a gnu,
And lots of things to see and do.

When I go to the zoo,
I'll watch the monkeys swinging by,
And tall giraffes
With their heads in the sky.
The sea lions playing in their pool,
And polar bears
Looking snowy white and cool.